by Roger Hurn & Jane A C West

Illustrated by Anthony Williams

Titles in Alien Detective Agency 2

Badger Publishing Limited
Oldmedow Road, Hardwick Industrial Estate,
King's Lynn PE30 4JJ
Telephone: 01438 791037
www.badgerlearning.co.uk

2 4 6 8 10 9 7 5 3 1

Spiders from the Stars ISBN 978-1-84926-944-5

First edition © 2012
This second edition © 2014

Text © Roger Hurn/Jane A C West 2012
Complete work © Badger Publishing Limited 2012

Publisher: Susan Ross
Senior Editor: Danny Pearson
Design: Julia King
Illustration: Anthony Williams

Contents

Vocabulary:

cyber squawk – alien version of tweeting

atmosphere – the envelope of gases surrounding the Earth or other planets; the mood created at an event

silicon – a non-metallic chemical element

planning permission – what you need from the council before you can build something

Main characters:

Jack Swift – the star of a top TV show

Wanda Darkstar – the Galactic Union's Alien Welfare Officer for Earth

Gorgonzola – Wanda's pet lunar mouse

Arakna – the Spider Queen of Araknid 5

Chapter 1

Wanda walked into the office of the Alien Detective Agency. She expected to see Jack sitting with his feet up on the desk as usual. But he wasn't. He was standing on the desk and shaking like a wet dog after a swim. "What's up?" she asked.

"It's a monster!" squealed Jack. "It's horrible, huge and hairy and it's out to get me."

Wanda whipped out her laser stun gun. "OK, Jack. Stay calm. I'll deal with it. Now, where exactly is this monster?"

Jack pointed with a trembling finger at a dark corner of the office.

Wanda frowned. She couldn't see anything there.

She grabbed a torch and shone it into the shadows. A very small and harmless-looking spider sat there minding its own business.

Wanda scooped it up and marched back to Jack. She held it out on the palm of her hand.

"Is this the horrible, huge, hairy monster you were on about?" she asked.

"Yes!" squeaked Jack. "I can't stand spiders."

Wanda closed her eyes and sighed. Then she stepped outside the office and put the spider down gently on the ground. The spider scuttled off. Wanda stepped back into the office.

Jack was still standing on the desk. "Has it gone?" he asked.

Wanda nodded. "Yes, it's safe to come down now."

Jack grinned and jumped down. "I wasn't scared of that spider," he said.

"Really?" said Wanda. "So why were you up on the desk?"

"It was for the spider's own safety," said Jack. "I was scared I'd tread on it by accident."

Wanda folded her arms. "No, you were just scared," she said.

Jack scowled. "Well, no one likes creepy-crawlies," he said, sulkily.

"That's a pity," said Wanda, "because the Galactic Union has just sent me a cyber squawk saying that the Spider Queen from Araknid 5 has landed in secret and is planning to hatch a vast swarm of spiders to take over the Earth."

Jack put his head in his hands. "That's bad news," he moaned.

"It is," agreed Wanda, "and it gets worse – the Galactic Union want us to stop her!"

Chapter 2

Silicon heart

Jack looked as nervous as a long-tailed cat in a room full of rocking chairs. "I'd love to come and help you sort out these spiders," he said, "but I've got to be somewhere else today."

Wanda folded her arms and tapped her foot. Jack knew this was a bad sign.

Then Wanda narrowed her eyes. Jack gulped. When Wanda folded her arms, tapped her foot and then narrowed her eyes to stare at him, he knew he was in big trouble.

"Where have you got to be?" Wanda's voice was colder than a penguin in a deep freeze.

Jack decided it was time to fib. "Er ... my fan club on the Moon is having a party today. I'm the guest of honour. And if I don't go it will spoil the atmosphere."

Jack gave Wanda his best Sci-Fi Spy Guy smile. Most people couldn't say no to him when he smiled that smile. But Wanda could. "There is no atmosphere on the Moon," she said. "So you can't spoil it by not being there."

Jack groaned. "You've got a heart made of stone," he said.

Wanda nodded. "Well, a heart made of silicon to be exact. Everybody on my home planet does. But that's because we're aliens – so get used to it!"

Jack suddenly brightened up. "Hey, that's why you can pick up spiders with your bare hands," he said. "Only aliens can do freaky stuff like that. But I'm 100 per cent human so that's why I can't do it." Jack laughed with relief. "So you see, I'm not a scaredy-cat after all!"

"Humans are so weird," thought Wanda. But she said, "Of course you're not a scaredy-cat, you're Sci-Fi Spy Guy. You laugh in the face of danger."

Jack nodded in agreement. "I do."

"And you laugh in the face of renegade robots and tentacled terrors."

"You bet I do," shouted Jack.

"And you laugh in the face of big fat spiders from Araknid 5."

"I so do!" yelled Jack. "Er... do I?"

"You do," said Wanda firmly. "Now come on, we need to get to the spider's web in the Forest of Gloom before she lays her eggs."

Chapter 3

The Forest of Gloom

The Forest of Gloom was a creepy place. The trees huddled close together as if they were plotting something nasty.

Branches brushed against Jack's face like ghostly fingers. He was as jumpy as a kangaroo on a trampoline. "I don't like it here, Wanda," he whispered. "It's a really gloomy place."

"That's why it's called the Forest of Gloom, not Sunshine Park," hissed Wanda, grumpily.

The truth was she didn't like the forest any more than Jack did. But Wanda wasn't going to admit it to him. After all, she was an alien with a heart of silicon, not a scaredy-cat TV actor who was afraid of spiders.

Then, suddenly, Wanda realised that Jack had a point. They had come to a clearing in the forest, and stretched across the trees was the biggest spider's web Wanda had ever seen.

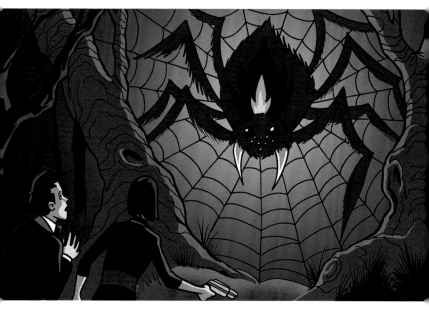

It had to be big because it was home to a spider so large it looked as if it could swallow a double-decker bus with one bite!

The hairy horror waved one of her eight legs at them. "Hello, Spy Guy," she said. "I'm Queen Arakna from Araknid 5. But who is your friend?"

Wanda took out her laser stun gun. "I'm Wanda Darkstar," she said. "And I'm arresting you for spinning a web without planning permission and for trying to take over the world."

The spider made a snuffling sound. She was laughing.

Suddenly, one of her long legs shot out and knocked the laser stun gun from Wanda's hand. "Good luck with arresting me," she said, as she grabbed Wanda and stuck her on her web!

Chapter 4

Jack's brain was shouting at his legs to run, but his legs weren't listening. "Hey, Arakna," he said, trying to sound as cool and relaxed as Sci-Fi Spy Guy. "I know Wanda can be a bit stuck-up sometimes, but that's going too far. So why don't you just unstick her and let her go?"

The giant spider looked at Wanda hanging helplessly on the web. "Well, I would, Spy Guy, but I'd like her to stick around for a bit longer."

Wanda tried to pull her arms and legs free but it was hopeless. "Run for your life, Jack!" she yelled. "Don't worry about me, I'll be fine."

Arakna leapt off the web. She landed next to Jack. "Yes, why don't you run, Spy Guy? I want some exercise to give me an appetite before I eat you. You and Wanda Darkstar will make a tasty snack and give me the energy I need to lay my eggs."

Jack's brain was down on its knees begging his legs to run, but they ignored it.

"Oh, you don't want to eat Wanda," said Jack.

"Why not?" asked the spider.

"She's got a silicon heart," replied Jack. "It would give you a tummy ache."

"Very well," replied the spider. "Then I shall just eat you!"

Chapter 5

Jack amazed himself by laughing in the face of danger. He thought he only did that on TV.

"Why do you want to eat me when I can give you something that you've always wanted?" he asked.

Arakna was curious. "What is that?"

"A beautiful wooden house," replied Jack.

The huge spider stared at him and Jack saw himself reflected in all her eyes. He liked what he saw. He gave himself his best Sci-Fi Spy Guy grin.

All ten reflections grinned back. "Wow! How cool is that!" he thought.

A hideous grinding noise snapped him back to reality. It was the spider's jaws. "Why do I want a house of wood when I have my web?" she asked.

Jack flung his arms out wide. "Duh! You're the Queen of the Spiders. You don't want to live in a web like any old spider. You need to live in a palace."

The spider nodded. "You're right, Spy Guy. I do need to live in a palace."

Jack smiled. "No problem, Queenie. I've got just the thing over here."

Jack led the spider to a woodman's hut on the other side of the clearing.

He opened the door and invited Arakna to go inside and take a look.

She refused. "This palace is far too small," she said. "I'll never squeeze inside it."

"Don't be silly," said Jack. "There's enough room for ten of you in there."

"Oh no, there isn't," said the spider.

"Oh yes, there is," said Jack.

"And I say there isn't!"

"So, why don't you prove it?" asked Jack.

"All right, I will," replied the huge spider.

She squeezed herself inside the hut, but one of her eight legs poked out. "See, I told you I wouldn't fit!"

"But you do," shouted Jack.

He leapt forward and shoved the spider's leg into the hut. Then he slammed the door shut and locked it.

Meanwhile, Wanda's pet lunar mouse, Gorgonzola, was chewing through the web to free her.

The sticky silk snapped. Wanda tumbled down and ran over to the shed.

She put her mouth to the keyhole and yelled, "Arakna, you're under arrest!"

Then she turned to Jack. "You did well for a scaredy-cat human," she said. "Maybe you've got a silicon heart after all!"

Facts about spiders

Spiders belong to a group of animals called arachnids.

A spider's body has two parts.

Spiders have eight legs but no wings or antennae.

Lots of people think that spiders are insects, but they aren't. Insects have six legs and three main body parts.

All spiders are predators and many will eat other spiders.

Spiders can bite but they can't chew.

All spiders produce silk, but not all spiders spin webs.

Spiders have oily bodies. This stops them from sticking to their own webs.

Male spiders are usually smaller than females.

All spiders have fangs! Luckily, most spider poison is too weak to harm humans.

Jack's joke

Q: What did the spider do with his new car?

He took it out for a spin!

Questions

Why is Jack standing on the desk?

How does Wanda deal with the spider?

What does Jack think is the reason why Wanda can pick up spiders with her bare hands and he can't?

What is Wanda's heart made of?

Where do Jack and Wanda go to find Queen Arakna?

What does Arakna do to Wanda?

Why does Arakna tell Jack to run?

What does Jack tell Arakna she needs?

How does Jack trick Arakna?

What does Wanda say about Jack's heart?